SO
BOY

Have you read these
Super Soccer Boy books?

⚽ Super Soccer Boy
and the Exploding Footballs

Super Soccer Boy
and the Evil Electronic Bunnies

 Super Soccer Boy
and the Snot Monsters

Super Soccer Boy ⚽
and the Giant Slugs

⚽ Super Soccer Boy
and the Alien Invasion

Super Soccer Boy
and the Laser Ray Robbery

⚽ Super Soccer Boy
and the Raging Robots

⚽

Coming Soon:
Super Soccer Boy
and the Monster Mutants

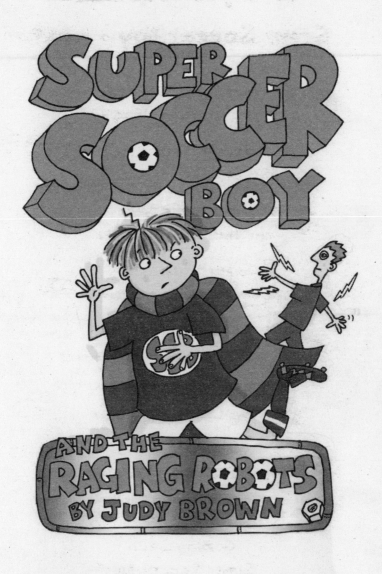

SUPER SOCCER BOY

AND THE RAGING ROBOTS

BY JUDY BROWN

Piccadilly Press • London

To the memory
of Ronald Searle

First published in Great Britain in 2012 by
Piccadilly Press Ltd, 5 Castle Road, London NW1 8PR
www.piccadillypress.co.uk

Text and illustration copyright © Judy Brown, 2012

ISBN: 978 1 84812 162 1

1 3 5 7 9 10 8 6 4 2

Printed and bound by CPI Group (UK) Ltd, Croydon, CR0 4YY

Design by Simon Davis
Cover illustration by Judy Brown

Chapter One

A Wicked Wembley Birthday

'Happy birthday, Harry!' called Jake.

He raced towards Harry, Harry's dad and two of their Little League teammates – Sanjay and Will – who were waiting for him outside Middletown station.

'Thanks, Jake!' said Harry,

'Right, that's all of us, then,' said Dad. 'Let's get on that platform and catch our train.'

As a birthday treat, Harry's dad was taking him and three friends to see a match at Wembley Stadium. It was summer half-term and a brand new tournament was being held for the sixteen European 'super' teams. All of the teams in the tournament had won leagues or cups in their own countries.

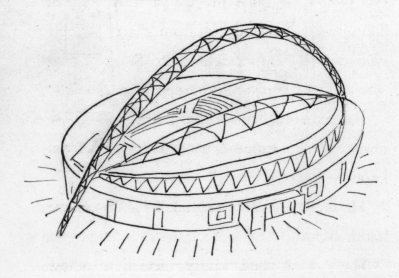

'This is going to be wicked!' said Sanjay. 'I've never been to Wembley before.'

'Me neither,' said Jake, equally excited.

Harry had. He'd seen the FA Cup Final at Wembley when he was sent VIP tickets for foiling the plot of evil Ernest Quigley. Quigley was the man who'd wanted to wipe football from the face of the earth with his custard-filled exploding footballs. It was the first of many evil plots Harry had foiled. Harry had been foiling evil plots ever since the day a freak bolt of lightning transformed him from 'Harry Gribble who couldn't even dribble' into Super Soccer Boy, and gave him amazing super soccer skills.

'I've been to Wembley,' said Harry, 'but I've never seen a European game before. Did you know —?'

'Here we go,' interrupted Will. 'It's footie statistic time.'

They all laughed. Harry seemed to know every fact that there was to know about football.

'I was just going to say,' Harry continued, 'that Emilio Pancetta, who's playing for RV today, has never ever been booked his whole career. He's won loads of fair play awards.'

'Wow – impressive!' said Sanjay.

'And he's played all over the world. He's one of my favourite players. I can't wait to see him play live,' said Harry dreamily.

At that moment, the train rumbled into the station.

'OK, boys,' said Harry's dad. 'Everybody on.'

After a pretty uneventful journey, they arrived at Wembley with plenty of time to browse the stadium store for souvenirs. Harry spent some of his birthday money on the biggest encyclopedia of football any of them had ever seen. Harry's dad was not too pleased about having to carry it around for the rest of the day. They each bought themselves a souvenir and then it was time to take their seats for the match.

The match was between Spanish team Athletico RV and little-known Latvian team FC Skronto. Little known to most people, that is – of course Harry knew all about them.

'Who *are* FC Skronto?' asked Jake. 'I've never heard of them.'

'Well,' Harry began, 'FC Skronto are a Latvian team, owned by Anton Antovich, who used to be a player himself. He was quite good too, till he got injured. He bought the team two years

ago after making a fortune out of caviar and electronics, and he's spent millions buying players to build up the team. Look, that's him in the programme.'

Harry pointed at a rather tall, dashing man wearing an incredibly expensive-looking suit and very shiny shoes.

Then, when he looked up, Harry spotted the man himself making his way to the owners' seats in the royal box, which was in the middle of the

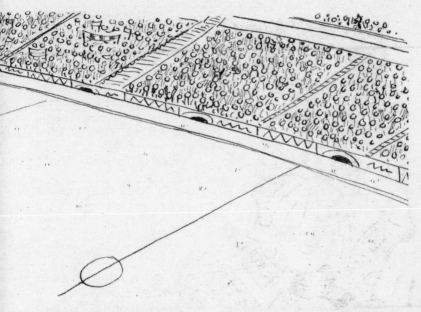

north stand. It was quite a way away, but since he became Super Soccer Boy, Harry's vision was amazing and he could see stuff other people needed binoculars to see.

'Here come the players!' exclaimed Will.

Both teams emerged from the tunnel and the crowd cheered and waved their flags excitedly.

'That's Pancetta, wearing number ten,' said Harry, almost jumping out of his seat with excitement. He pointed to one of the RV players.

Harry wasn't the only Pancetta fan. As Pancetta warmed up with keepy-uppies, the crowd cheered his every movement. At least they did to begin with, but Pancetta seemed to be having trouble controlling the ball and it was spilling all over the place.

'He doesn't look that great,' said Will.

'Maybe he's injured,' said Harry, concerned.

Soon it was time for the game to start and the players moved into their positions on the pitch.

'This is so exciting!' said Sanjay, grinning from ear to ear.

Chapter Two

Tournament Trouble

PEEP!

The referee blew his whistle and the match kicked off.

'Come on, Athletico!' shouted Harry, pleased when they won the ball and immediately threatened the FC Skronto goal.

'RV! RV! RV!' chanted his friends, joining Harry in cheering for the Spanish team.

'They're amazing,' said Jake.

Harry glanced at Antovich, Skronto's owner. He did not look happy.

'It's all too much for Skronto,' said Harry's dad.

A huge cheer welled up from the crowd as Athletico surged forward towards the Skronto goal.

'Look!' said Harry. 'Pancetta's completely unmarked. This has one-nil written all over it.'

Will started to commentate as though he was on TV. '. . . and Pancetta makes a run for goal – he's completely unchallenged – there's no one between him and the goalkeeper. Sanchez passes to Pancetta – the keeper's beaten – it's going to be an easy goal for Athletico RV . . . Oh!'

A huge 'Oh' of disappointment echoed around the stadium. Pancetta had missed from a few metres away from the goal!

'Impossible!' said Harry, stunned by the

terrible shot. 'That was the worst miss ever in the history of football.' Let's face it, Harry would know.

The Skronto keeper, Heinrich, kicked the ball back into play, but Athletico continued to pile on the pressure. Eventually it was too much for the Latvian team and Heinrich made a bad mistake and let the ball in. RV, deservedly, were one-nil up.

'Oh no!' said Jake. 'Right between the legs! How embarrassing.'

Harry looked over at Antovich – he was purple with rage.

When the game kicked off again after the goal, it was Skronto's turn to put on the pressure.

'This is turning into a great match,' said Sanjay. 'End to end stuff!'

Then something extraordinary happened. Pancetta went charging up the pitch after the Skronto striker.

'What's Pancetta doing?' said Harry. 'He's . . .'

As Harry spoke, Pancetta brought the Skronto striker down with a blatant foul just outside the penalty area. There was a collective gasp from the crowd.

'What the —?' said Harry horrified, just like everyone else.

'He's got to get booked for that,' said Jake as the referee marched purposefully towards Pancetta. The Skronto player writhed around on the ground, going for an Oscar for best supporting actor.

'At least!' said Will.

But things got worse than that.

The referee took the cards out of his pocket and flashed the yellow card dramatically into the air. Then something even more unexpected happened. Pancetta snatched the card out of the ref's hand and ran off. The referee chased after him, madly blowing his whistle. But Pancetta turned around and started blowing raspberries and making silly faces and gestures. The whole of the stadium began to laugh. Well, it did look pretty funny.

Harry wasn't laughing though. 'What is he doing? He's going to get himself sent off!'

Sure enough, when the referee caught up, out came the red card and, for the first time in his career, Pancetta had not only been booked, but sent off too! Harry was speechless.

With their star player off the pitch in such bizarre circumstances, the rest of the Athletico team lost their way. Skronto took advantage of the extra man and managed to scrape a two-one victory.

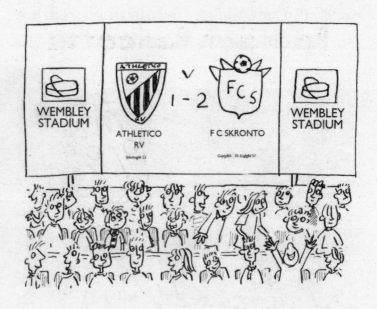

Chapter Three

Peculiar Pancetta

'Thanks, Mr Gribble, that was brilliant,' Jake said to Harry's dad on the way home from the match.

'Glad you enjoyed it,' said Harry's dad. 'How about you, Harry?'

'Yeah, it was great,' said Harry quietly. He stared

17

out of the train window and they could all tell that his birthday treat had been partly spoilt by the behaviour of one of his footballing heroes.

'I'm going to watch the highlights later to see if I can spot myself in the crowd,' said Sanjay.

'Me too,' said Will.

And me, thought Harry, but only because he still couldn't believe what he'd seen.

They dropped his friends off and then went home. After dinner, cake and party games with Harry's little sister Daisy, Harry sat on the sofa with Ron, his pet rat, to watch the highlights on TV. Unlike his friends, it wasn't just to try and spot his face in the crowd.

'You're not going to believe this, Ron – Pancetta went crazy.'

Everything happened just as he remembered and he still couldn't believe it. Neither could the other players.

'Look at their faces, Ron,' said Harry.

Just then, the camera shot changed briefly to show the royal box where Antovich and Athletico's owner Pedro Palomo were sitting. While Palomo's face was a picture of shock, Antovich, who moments before had been purple with rage, looked like he was actually laughing.

'Huh!' grunted Harry.

After the highlights, there was a short interview with Pancetta.

'What have you got to say about your red card today, Emilio?' asked the reporter. 'After all those years with not even a booking, what happened?'

'What happened, what happened, I play football and . . .' His left eye twitched violently. '. . . I sent off and what happened?'

'Er, yes,' the reporter went on, a little puzzled. 'And what do you have to say to your fans?'

'Fans. Say to your fans — say hello to your

fans,' said Emilio, glassy-eyed. His eye twitched again.

'Er, thank you, Emilio,' said the reporter.

'A bit of a language problem there, I think!' said Barry Spinaker in the studio. 'But very uncharacteristic behaviour from a great player.'

'You're not kidding,' agreed Harry. 'He has to be ill or something, eh, Ron?'

'Now let's look at tomorrow's fixtures,' said Barry.

'Yes, let's!' said Harry, cheering up.

There were two matches scheduled for the next day, one at twelve o'clock and one at four.

'That's my day sorted then, Ron. A whole day of watching football! Sweeeeet!'

Chapter Four

Butter Fingers

The next day at eleven forty-five, Harry was sitting on the sofa with his statistic logs, his new encyclopedia, three packets of crisps, a fizzy drink and Ron, ready for the start of the match. The match wasn't at Wembley this time but at the Millenium Stadium in Cardiff.

'Welcome to *Soccer Scene*!' said Barry Spinaker introducing the show. 'And in a moment it's the match between Italian Pizza Cup winners Prego, and Russian champions Smolgograd.'

'Definitely the underdogs, Ron. Prego should win this easily,' said Harry.

'Smolgograd are definitely regarded as the underdogs in this match,' said Barry. 'With Prego's team of stars and international keeper Mauro Moldi in goal, it will be a very difficult game for the Russian team.'

'Safest pair of hands in the game, Moldi,'
Harry told Ron. 'He hasn't let a goal in for
seventy matches, not even a penalty! That's
nearly two whole seasons in the Italian league
and internationals. He's awesome.'

Well, he had been.

As soon as the game kicked off, Moldi's
nightmare began. He played so badly, it was
almost as if he was diving the wrong way on
purpose, and after half an hour, Prego were
already four goals down.

'What on earth is going on?!' exclaimed Harry, after the fourth goal hit the back of the net.

Their manager, Maximo Grande, was clearly thinking the same thing and the second goalkeeper was speedily warming up on the touchline, while the fourth official held up the substitute board to call Moldi off the pitch.

'Moldi has just seen that his manager wants to substitute him. I can't say it's a surprise – he's having a shocking time out there,' said the commentator. 'But what's this? He's ignoring the substitution . . . He's . . . he's sitting down in the middle of the goal mouth!'

'What *is* he doing?' said Harry.

The commentator carried on. 'And now the rest of the team are standing around him. Maximo is telling Moldi to get off the pitch, and here comes the referee. He's shown him a red card, he's sending Moldi off, for obstruction presumably. Is Moldi going? He's getting up . . .

but . . . what is he doing now?!'

Moldi ran over to the corner flag and pulled it right out of the ground.

'He's gone crazy!' said Harry.

There was more to come. Moldi ran towards the referee waving the flag around and the referee turned and fled down the pitch with Moldi charging after him, still waving the flag.

Three of the Prego players joined the chase, trying to get Moldi to stop. It took all three of them to rugby-tackle Moldi to the ground.

'I've never seen anything like it!' said the commentator. 'What dreadful behaviour from a player that so many youngsters look up to.'

'Quite!' said Harry, flabbergasted.

Four stewards came on and escorted Moldi off the pitch and straight down the tunnel.

'I wouldn't be surprised if that was the last we'll see of Moldi in this tournament,' the commentator said dramatically. 'It's the kind of behaviour that must be stamped out of football altogether. If youngsters see professionals setting this sort of example . . .' He started droning on about the old days when players showed more respect, and Harry stopped listening.

After ten minutes of injury time, the half-time whistle blew. Just after that, Harry spotted a helicopter flying away from the stadium. Harry looked at the logo on the side.

'That's the Antovich Inc logo,' he said. 'I'm sure. It's the logo that Skronto wear on their shirts. I guess it's Antovich's helicopter. He must have been at the match. I wonder why he's leaving at half-time – business to do, I s'ppose.'

Meanwhile, in the helicopter, Anton Antovich was rubbing his hands together with glee. He sat back in his seat and smiled smugly.

THE VERY NEXT SEASON, ANTOVICH'S TEAM DID THE LEAGUE AND CUP DOUBLE WITHOUT HIM!

IT'S SO UNFAIR.

HE WAS SO GUTTED, HE TURNED HIS BACK ON FOOTBALL FOR YEARS.

FIRST HE WENT TO UNIVERSITY AND STUDIED ELECTRONICS WHICH HE'D ALWAYS ENJOYED,

FISH EGGS

AND THEN HE TOOK OVER THE FAMILY'S CAVIAR BUSINESS. IT TURNED OUT...

...ANTOVICH WAS EVEN BETTER AT BUSINESS THAN HE WAS AT FOOTBALL, SO GOOD IN FACT THAT SOON...

SALES

HE WAS RICH ENOUGH TO BUY HIS OWN FOOTBALL CLUB!

TO HELP WITH TRAINING, ANTOVICH BUILT A FOOTBALL KICKING ROBOT. IT WAS SO EFFECTIVE THAT HE STARTED SELLING THEM TO OTHER CLUBS...

HIS OWN CLUB, F. C. SKRONTO WASN'T VERY GOOD AND IT WAS DIFFICULT TO PERSUADE THE BEST PLAYERS TO SIGN, EVEN THOUGH HE COULD PAY THEM WELL.

I NEED TO BUILD UP THE TEAM.

AND THAT WAS WHEN HE HAD AN EVEN BETTER IDEA...

WHAT IF I COULD BUILD A ROBOT PLAYER, GOOD ENOUGH TO PLAY OUT ON PITCH?

Chapter Five

Stupid Strikers

Harry was going to watch the next game with
Jake. Before it started, he and Ron went to the
park – Harry was going to play kickabout with
Jake. Jake hadn't seen the match earlier, so Harry
filled him in on what had happened.

'It was crazy,' he said. 'It was almost as if Moldi threw the game away on purpose.'

'Weird after yesterday, and the way that Pancetta went loopy,' said Jake. 'I wonder if anything funny will happen in the next match.'

Harry was wondering the same thing.

'Who's playing?' asked Jake.

'It's Soderberg – they're the Swedish champions – against United FC. Should be a close one,' said Harry, heading the ball to himself as he ran backwards and forwards. It was making Jake and Ron feel seasick. 'It's nearly four – we should get back to your place.'

'Ready when you are,' said Jake.

They got back just as the match was about to kick off. Harry was right, of course – it was very close from the start.

'Did you know . . .' Harry began.

Jake prepared himself for some more of Harry's football stats.

'. . . that both teams have two star strikers and between them this season they've scored over a hundred goals?'

'Fascinating,' said Jake, wondering if he'd ever score that many, and how many more than that Harry had scored that season.

The commentator was clearly enjoying the match. 'This is gripping end to end stuff,' he said. 'Both teams are at the top of their game.'

He got even more excited when United

scored. 'GOOOOOAAAALLLLLAAAA!' he boomed.

Harry and Jake looked at each other and burst out laughing.

Three goals later it was half-time and the teams went in all square at two–all. There was the usual half-time stuff with ex-football players talking about the game so far and pretty soon the crowd were going back to their seats for the second half.

'Look!' said Harry. 'It's Antovich again!'

'Oh? Where?' asked Jake.

'There, in the executive box. He's on his mobile. He was watching the earlier game too – I saw his helicopter.'

'He must be going to every game,' said Jake. 'Bet you wish you could do that!'

'Yeah, it helps if you have a helicopter though,' Harry said, laughing.

The second half kicked off and on the pitch trouble kicked off too. Two of the opposing strikers began to argue.

'Oh, here we go, looks like there's going to be trouble,' said Jake.

He wasn't wrong.

One player pushed the other, who pushed back. He poked him in the stomach, the other poked back. Then they started kicking each other in the shins, followed by hair pulling, and moments later they were rolling around on the ground. It was like watching a fight in a nursery school!

'What is happening to our game of football?' wailed the commentator melodramatically. 'What kind of behaviour is this?'

Their teammates were beginning to join in now and the referee did brilliantly to stop it all from turning into a major fight. Needless to say, the two strikers were sent off, but they were still trying to attack each other even as four burly security guards dragged them from the pitch.

'Why did they start a fight in the first place?' asked Jake.

'I dunno,' said Harry. 'I didn't see anything happen. Did you?'

'What mystifies me, Barry,' said the commentator, 'is what sparked off the argument in the first place. Let's look at some replays.'

However many times they watched, from whatever angle, there seemed to be no reason at all why the strikers had started to fight.

'This is getting really weird,' said Harry.

After all the fuss had died down and the game

restarted, Harry saw Antovich's helicopter fly away from the ground.

'He's leaving early again,' said Harry.

'Maybe he disapproves of all the bad behaviour,' Jake suggested.

'Maybe,' said Harry, but deep down his Super Soccer Boy senses told him that something dodgy was going on.

Chapter Six

Something Fishy

Harry had a restless night filled with dreams about referees and red cards. In one of them it was Harry being sent off because he'd taken a giant Ron to play in his team and the opposition were too frightened to play.

When he went down to breakfast, Dad had just finished reading the newspaper. It was full of stories about the tournament and the sending offs.

'I think it's disgraceful, really I do,' said Mum. 'They get paid all that money, and they behave like two year olds.'

It was hard for Harry to disagree. He got himself a bowl of cereal with extra flakes for Ron, and sat at the table and flicked through the paper. It was full of interviews with 'experts' of one kind and another – ex-football players and officials.

'I know,' said Dad. 'Like Nobby Charlston says, players in his day showed some respect. I don't know what these so-called stars are playing at.'

Harry, still busy looking at the newspaper, had spotted an interview with Mauro Moldi's wife. Her words made Harry's super soccer senses tingle even more.

'Mauro hasn't been himself at all this past week,' she said. 'He's not been eating and he never seems to sleep. He's just up all night plugged into his laptop or on his mobile. He was never like that before.'

'Not himself, eh?' said Harry, thoughtfully.

MOLDI NOT HIMSELF SAYS HIS WIFE

'What did you say, Harry?' asked Mum.

'Oh nothing, just talking to myself,' he replied.

'First sign of madness, Harry!' Dad chuckled.

On the opposite page, there was a quote from Antovich.

'It's all very disappointing. Fair play and discipline are such an important part of the game and I haven't seen enough of either in this tournament.'

'Hmmm,' said Harry, 'and you've been to every match, or at least part of every match.' *But why only part?* Harry was beginning to wonder. Could there be a connection between Antovich and the strange behaviour? *I need to do some Googling,* he thought.

Harry went into the living room, booted up the computer and typed *Antovich* into the search box.

AntInc.com was at the top of the list of results and Harry clicked on it. An impressive, shiny website opened up with a list of menus relating to both sides of the Antovich business.

'Ah, let's try this!' said Harry clicking on a button marked *Research Projects*. Harry was taken to a new page with a new set of menus. He read them out to himself: 'Sports science, fish breeding, conservation, ah . . . robotics. Now that sounds interesting.'

He clicked on the link.

The page that opened showed photos of glass buildings, which were seemingly some sort of research facility, and other photos of various bits of electronic equipment. There was a box in which was written:

**THIS PART OF THE SITE IS
UNDER CONSTRUCTION.
ANTOVICH INCORPORATED IS CURRENTLY
INVESTING IN AN EXCITING PROGRAMME
OF EXPERIMENTAL ROBOTICS.**

'Very fishy,' said Harry, 'and I'm not talking about the caviar.'

The first thing Harry did after his discovery was to ring Jake.

'Hey, Harry, what's up?'

'We've got some work to do,' said Harry. 'I don't think Antovich is all he seems.'

Here we go, thought Jake. 'And what exactly do you suppose we should do?'

'I've been thinking about that.'

'Yes, I thought you might have,' said Jake.

'Meet me outside Middletown football

ground at eight o'clock tomorrow morning. We're going on a trip!'

Harry knew this was a job for Super Soccer Boy!

Chapter Seven

Stowaways

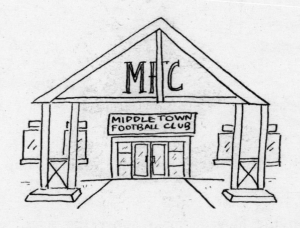

Next morning when Jake arrived at Middletown FC, Harry was already waiting outside.

'Hi, Harry,' he said. 'So what's the plan?'

'Well, you know there's a trip to the next tournament game at Wembley?'

'I do now,' said Jake.

Harry pointed to an empty coach in the car park. 'We're going to stowaway on the coach.'

'But they'll see us, Harry. It's not like a ship or something.'

'In the luggage racks above the seats,' said Harry. 'I've been on the coach before. The luggage racks have doors you pull down. There's loads of room in them. It'll be just like being in the top bunk in a caravan.'

'Sounds lovely,' said Jake sarcastically, thinking how not lovely it sounded.

'We've got to get on before anyone else arrives,' Harry said.

'But it's locked, isn't it?' asked Jake.

'Good job I've got the key, then!' Harry smiled, holding it up.

'And how did you get that? Or don't I want to know?'

'Got here early and went through the window up there with my Utility Boots.'

Harry had designed his own boots when he first became Super Soccer Boy. They had all sorts of different modes from *Skate* to *Turbo* and *Hover*.

He pointed to a window on the third floor of the clubhouse. 'They always leave the loo window open, and the office where they keep the keys for the coach is just down the corridor. Shocking security.'

'I doubt very much they were expecting anyone to be wearing special boots that would let them fly through the air,' said Jake.

'Fair point,' said Harry. 'I'll put the keys back when we've unlocked the coach and they'll just think someone forgot to lock it last time it was used.'

'What if someone wants to use the luggage racks we're in?'

'Thought of that too.' Harry held up two signs printed out from his computer.

OUT OF ORDER

DO NOT OPEN
UNDER ANY
CIRCUMSTANCES

'And I've got a camping mat for each compartment to make them more comfy.'

'You think of everything, Harry!' said Jake.

'I do my best.' Harry grinned.

Everything went to plan and as the coach set off, Harry and Jake were lying comfortably – well, relatively comfortably – on opposite sides of the coach, although Jake did feel a bit like a sardine in a tin.

About an hour later, they arrived at the ground and once everyone was off the coach, Harry and Jake emerged, a little crumpled, out of the luggage rack.

'Right,' said Harry as he looked around at the stewards manning the entrance gates. 'You'll have to create a diversion so I can get inside.'

'Er, like what exactly?' Jake asked nervously.

'Erm ... pretend you came with your dad and you've lost him. You can cry and everything.'

Why do I always get myself into this? thought Jake.

'I'll whizz in and find a way to get you in too,' said Harry.

'O ... K ...' said Jake trying to remember what the teacher always said when they did drama. *Keep it real.* Yes, that was it.

Jake walked towards the entrance and started

to wail. He even managed to squeeze out a tear.

The lady at the entrance gate ran over to see what was the matter and as she did, Harry used his super soccer speed to whizz in behind her and vault over the turnstile. Once  inside, it didn't take him long to find a large storage cupboard with a couple of stewards' jackets with *Wembley Stadium Staff* embroidered on them. He also grabbed some caps for them to pull over their faces in case anyone looked a little too closely and wondered why the stadium was hiring such young-looking stewards.

'Excellent!' he said. 'Now to get Jake in.'

Outside, a small crowd had gathered around the

distraught boy who had lost his dad. They were asking all sorts of questions.

'Where did you last see him?'

'What was he wearing?'

'What's your name, son?'

Just then Jake's mobile went off. 'Er, hello, Har— I mean, Dad. Oh right, yes, I'll meet you there. Some nice people have been looking after me.' Jake smiled at them angelically and rang off. 'That was my dad,' he lied. 'I'm meeting him at the side entrance. Thank you, everyone.'

'You're welcome, son,' said the lady from the gate, patting him kindly on the shoulder. *What a nice, polite boy*, she thought.

Everyone went back to what they had been doing and Jake dashed off to meet Harry.

'Here!' said Harry, waiting by some recycling bins. 'Put this on.' He handed Jake a steward's jacket.

'It's a bit big,' said Jake.

'Yeah, I know, but there are so many people around we should get away with it. Just try and look tall,' said Harry.

'That's dumb, Harry.'

'Whatever, follow me.' Harry giggled. 'The staff entrance is this way.'

Fortunately, as Harry had said, there were enough people going in and out for them not to be noticed and they shuffled in the staff entrance. As they did, Harry spotted something.

'Look! That must be Antovich's limo. It's got the company logo on the side.'

The car pulled up outside the executive entrance and Antovich got out and went into the ground.

'Quick, we have to follow him to his seat,' said Harry.

'I wonder why he came by car and not helicopter this time?' said Jake.

'He's got some sort of big mansion near London, I think,' Harry said. 'Too close to need the helicopter, I guess – or maybe he just wanted a change.'

Staying far enough away not to be spotted by Antovich, they flashed their staff jackets at security and followed him to the executive stand and waited at the back while he took his seat.

The players were already on the pitch.

PEEP!

The game kicked off and Harry did his best not to let the play distract him from watching Antovich. It wasn't easy.

The match was between Pretzel, the Austrian champions, and the French side, Camembert, and it was full of action from the start.

It wasn't long though before Harry's attention

was attracted by something else. Antovich was using his mobile. That wasn't odd at all, but what was odd was that the picture on the mobile — which Harry could clearly see with his super soccer vision — was a player-level view of the pitch.

He watched as Antovich pressed a sequence of numbers. On the pitch, Bobbolin, Pretzel's star player, seemed to deliberately hand ball.

'It's Bobbolin!' whispered Harry.

'Yes I know,' said Jake. 'He just hand-balled.'

'No, I know that. But I think Antovich made him do it somehow. His phone is showing Bobbolin's view of the pitch!'

Antovich tapped more numbers on his phone and Bobbolin went crazy.

He shoved the ball up his shirt and ran around the pitch trying to pull other players' shorts down. Harry could see by the way his whole body was shaking that Antovich was laughing.

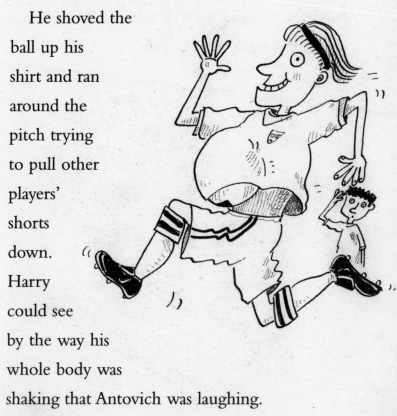

Bobbolin ran to one of the goals, climbed up the net and balanced along the bar doing ballet steps. There was total mayhem on the pitch and the crowd was rolling around in hysterics.

Then Antovich turned off his phone, put it back in his pocket and got up to leave.

Chapter Eight

Antovich's Antics

'Quick!' said Harry. 'Follow him!'

Harry and Jake ran down the steps and followed Antovich as he made his way towards the stadium exit. They could see his limo waiting outside.

'Wait for me by the coach, Jake, I'm going to follow the car.'

'But —' Jake was just about to ask him how, when he realised that Harry was still wearing his Utility Boots.

The limousine sped away from the ground. Harry put his Utility Boots into *Turbo* mode and followed, whizzing through the traffic, trying hard not to be seen in Antovich's rear view mirror.

After about twenty minutes' high speed whizzing, Harry arrived just behind the limousine

at a huge mansion with electric security gates. The gates opened as the car approached. It drove sedately inside and the gates closed behind.

'So this is where you live,' said Harry to himself. 'Not a million miles away from Middletown as it happens.' He began to do a circuit of the wall outside the grounds, but it was a big place. He glanced at his watch. 'No more time for this now,' he said to himself. 'I'd better get back to Jake. But tomorrow, when you're at the next match, I'll be here!'

Harry turned around and zoomed back to Wembley to catch the coach. It was just about to leave.

'It's too late,' said Jake as Harry arrived. 'Everyone's already on the coach – they'll see us.'

'Luggage compartment under the seats, quick! It opens from the outside.'

They wrenched the door open between them and clambered in.

'We'd better wedge it open a bit in case we can't get out,' Harry said.

Jake looked alarmed.

'It's OK, it'll be fine.'

'Hmmm,' said Jake, 'you've said that before.'

It *was* fine though, even if they had a very bumpy, smelly and uncomfortable journey back to Middletown.

Feeling a little battered and bruised, Harry and Jake climbed out of the luggage compartment and walked home from Middletown FC.

'I'm going back to the mansion tomorrow, when Antovich is at the next match. Coming?' asked Harry.

'Er, well . . .' Jake was unsure.

'It'll be OK. He won't be there. He's been at every match so far – I think he has to be close to the action.'

'Er . . . I . . .'

Harry smiled encouragingly and Jake, as usual, found it hard to say no. 'Oh all right!' he said.

'Great!' said Harry. 'I'll cycle round for you in the morning.'

Harry got home and switched on the TV to find

the sports channel. They were still talking about the appalling behaviour on pitch.

'So it's FC Skronto who are in line for the fair play award. And the rumour is that the value of these offending players in the transfer market has been badly affected by their behaviour. Is that true, Barry?'

'Absolutely!' said Barry Spinaker. 'There's been a marked drop in the value of both Pancetta and Moldi. Part of their appeal has been how incredibly reliable they've always been – but their reputation is now in tatters. And with their contracts up for renewal next season, if these events aren't just a one off, we could even be talking about free transfers.'

'Wow!' said Harry. 'I bet I know who'd be offering to take them on. I wonder if that's part of Antovich's plan.'

Antovich had been watching the same news report . . .

AHA! LOVELY FREE PLAYERS FOR MY TEAM OR AT LEAST HALF PRICE ONES. THE MORE MONEY I SAVE ON PLAYERS, THE MORE PLAYERS I CAN **BUY!**

HIS PLAN WAS WORKING BEAUTIFULLY...

WITH THE BEST TEAMS LOSING THEIR STAR PLAYERS, EVERYTHING WAS SET UP FOR ANTOVICH TO GET HIS FIRST EVER TROPHY FOR HIS SHINY NEW TROPHY CABINET.

EMPTY

EMPTY

IT WAS ANTOVICH'S DREAM OF WINNING A TROPHY WHICH HAD MADE HIM HATCH **HIS EVIL PLAN...**

USING HIS PROGRAMMING SKILLS, ROBOTICS EXPERTISE AND 3D IMAGING, HE CREATED REPLICAS OF SOME OF THE WORLD'S GREATEST PLAYERS.

THEY WERE SO REALISTIC, YOU COULDN'T TELL THEM APART!

NOW ALL I HAVE TO DO IS SWAP THEM WITH THE REAL PLAYERS...

BUT HOW?

IT DIDN'T TAKE LONG FOR HIM TO THINK OF A PLAN.

Chapter Nine

Science Fiction, Science Fact!

The following day, Harry packed his backpack.

'Utility Boots, football, Ron – never know when I might need you.'

The next scheduled match in the tournament was at four o'clock, so just after

lunch Harry cycled over to Jake's house. 'Ready, Jake?' Jake was stuffing the remains of a chicken salad sandwich into his mouth. 'OK.' *Chomp, chomp.* 'Coming.'

Harry showed Jake a map of their route. 'It's quite a long way,' said Harry.

'You're not kidding. Hang on a minute.' Jake dashed back inside and emerged a minute later with four packets of crisps and two bottles of water. 'Supplies,' he said, shoving them in his backpack. 'We'll be hungry after all that cycling.'

Harry grinned – as always with Jake, food was a top priority.

★ ★ ★

After a long ride, they eventually arrived at Antovich's mansion and hid their bikes in some bushes outside.

'That's a big wall,' said Jake. 'How on earth do we get over it?'

'Do you really need to ask?' said Harry, taking his Utility Boots out of his bag and swapping them with his trainers. 'Hop on! It's piggyback time.'

Jake did as he was told and Harry, with Jake onboard, rose gently over the wall and landed softly on the other side.

'Look!' said Harry. In the grounds of the mansion stood the glass buildings he had seen on the Antovich Inc website. 'That's where we should start – I think it's his research facility.'

There was a security guard's booth near the gate but the guard seemed to be far too interested watching his TV to notice Harry and Jake. They sneaked over to the glass building and tried the door.

'It's locked!' said Harry, rattling it hard.

'Yeah, look – here's a keypad with numbers on it. We're going to need a code.'

'Hmmm, now what would that be, I wonder?' Harry mused.

'Date of birth?' suggested Jake. 'Whatever that is.'

'Easy,' said Harry. 'Too easy probably, but worth a try.'

Harry tried all possible combinations of Antovich's date of birth, month first, day first, all four numbers of the year, then just two. No luck.

'It could be anything,' said Jake. 'We're stuffed.'

'Not yet.' Harry thought hard. 'What numbers would he choose? Something footbally, I'll bet. What would a football player be most likely to pick ... I wonder ...' He typed in 1, 0, 9, 5. There were three short beeps and the door slid open with a satisfying *whoosh*.

'Brilliant!' said Jake, impressed. 'How did you know what to type in?'

'His shirt number on pitch and the number of goals he scored as a professional player. Simple really,' Harry said a little smugly.

'Well, who would have thought all that nerdy knowledge of yours would prove so useful!' Jake said, smiling.

'OK, let's go,' said Harry and walked into the building.

Inside, they found themselves in a large foyer with halls and doorways leading off from it.

There didn't seem to be anybody around. Harry picked a door, walked over and opened it.

'WOW!' he said. 'Jake, come and look at this.'

The room was full of robots, suspended from the ceiling in rows. Not the toy, shooting, rotating-body kind of robots. It was like a scene from a science fiction film, or to be entirely accurate, from *I, Robot*! They were silver-coloured and obviously based on the human figure.

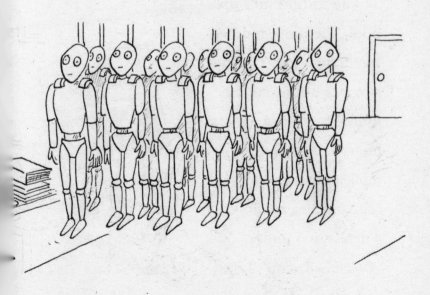

'Awesome!' said Jake. It certainly was. Harry rummaged through some papers on a workbench. 'Hey, Jake, come here.' He was looking at a book of diagrams and schematics for more advanced robots or 'androids'.

The further into the book, the more finished the designs got. The last two pages showed the finished product – a pretty convincing replica human, with skin, hair, everything. There was another book filled with photos of football players taken

from every conceivable angle. They included a
load of Pancetta. That was when they spotted
some finished versions of the human replica
robots on the other side of the room.

'Look!' said Harry. 'Isn't that Claus Turnip, the
guy who plays for Santa Pinto?! Hey, Jake. That's
what he's up to!' Harry exclaimed.

'What?' asked Jake.

'Antovich is replacing
football players with robots
and controlling them. That's
why he's been at
the matches. He
controls them
with his
mobile!'

'My God, I
think you're
right!' said Jake,
taking a closer look at Claus Turnip's robot
version. 'You'd never know though, not to look

at them. That they were robots, I mean.'

'What was that?' said Harry, startled.

'I didn't hear anything,' said Jake, looking rather worried.

'There it is again,' said Harry, trying to tune his super soccer hearing – it was so acute that he could detect movement anywhere on the pitch – to try and identify the sound and where it was coming from. 'It sounds like people playing indoor five-a-side football, and it's coming from . . . downstairs.'

Chapter Ten

A Room Full of Stars

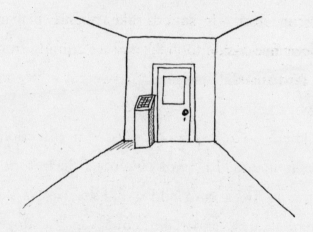

Harry followed the sounds and Jake followed Harry. He led Jake out of the room and down a corridor. Through the door at the end of the corridor, they could see stairs leading to a lower level.

'There's another keypad,' said Jake.

'Let's hope it has the same code,' said Harry, punching it in.

They were both relieved when the door opened with a click. Now Jake could hear what Harry had been listening to. It sounded almost like a game of football, being played by people of several nationalities, judging by the accents.

'Over 'ere! On de 'ed,' said a slightly Italian-sounding voice.

'It's Pancetta!' said Harry. 'I swear it is!' He ran down the stairs.

There was a vast room, divided into sections, which included a mini cinema, a dormitory, a living room, a gym and a full size five-a-side pitch! Harry and Jake could see a dozen international players watching or taking part in a lively training game. All of them were wearing the FC Skronto kit. Some had bibs to show which side they were on.

'Look, there's Pancetta,' said Harry, thrilled to

see what he now knew was his *real* favourite
player. 'And there's Moldi in goal and over there
is Bobbolin and all the players who have been
sent off so far.' The others, Harry suspected, were
those Antovich had yet to get sent off.

'Er . . . hello!' he said, a bit embarrassed and more than a little starstruck. 'Excuse me!' he called a little louder.

Moldi, who was in goal at the end nearest Harry, was the first to notice him. He caught the ball expertly off the next attempted shot and pointed up at Harry.

'Can we help you, young man?' asked Bobbolin politely.

'Er, I think it's the other way round,' said Harry. 'We're here to help you. May I come down and speak with you all?'

'Certainly. Would you like some autographs?' asked Pancetta.

'Er, not exactly!' said Harry.

At the football tournament, a remote alarm had alerted Antovich to the break in.

'So someone has used my code, have they?' he said. 'Let's take a look.'

He accessed the security cameras in the basement of the research building. 'So! Super Soccer Boy. Caught like a rat in a trap. And I see

you have a friend with you. Looks like I'll have a chance to try out my junior robot version sooner than I expected. MWWAHAHAHA!'

He glanced down at the action on the pitch. 'Just need to finish up here first.'

Antovich punched in a few buttons, and instantly Tortellini approached the referee, stole his whistle and ran from one end of the pitch to the other, blowing it like a mad man. Then he grabbed the substitute board from the referee's assistant, typed something rude on it and held it up to the crowd.

'There, that's done. OK, Dimitri,' he said into his mobile. 'Get the limo ready – I'm leaving.'

Chapter Eleven

Lock Down

'Hi,' said Harry. 'He's Jake, this is Ron and I'm Harry.'

'Otherwise known as Super Soccer Boy!' added Jake.

'Super who?!' asked Peter Slouch of United FC.

'Why don't you show him, Harry?' said Jake.

Harry couldn't resist it. 'OK if I join in?' he asked.

The players smiled.

'Be our guest,' said Slouch.

So Harry put the rest of his kit on and joined the game.

Ten minutes later, after a display of his awesome soccer skills, they all stood speechless.

'Very impressive, young Harry,' said Bobbolin. 'You will go far.'

'Thanks,' said Harry, blushing. 'But what are you all doing here? You know you're supposed to be playing in the Euro tournament.'

'Tournament? What tournament?' asked Slouch.

'You don't remember?' said Jake.

'We're in a special experimental training environment for our team, FC Skronto,' Bobbolin informed them.

'But none of you are signed to Skronto, at least not yet,' said Harry.

'Of course we are – look,' said Slouch. He went over to the cinema area and pressed a big red button. A weird electronic sound filled the room and a coloured spiral swirled onto the screen.

Instantly, every player was drawn to the spiral. They walked slowly to the two rows of chairs and sat down. Once they were seated, flashing images of the players wearing Skronto kit replaced the swirly shape.

'Antovich has brainwashed them, Jake,' said Harry.

He ran over and switched off the screen.

'No, no, no, this is all wrong!' shouted Harry.

'Pancetta, you play for Athletico RV and you,' he looked at Moldi, 'you've been with Prego for four seasons!'

They looked at him blankly.

'Show them on your phone, Harry,' said Jake.

'Great idea! Look, maybe if you see what's been happening, you'll remember who you really play for.'

Harry searched the internet on his phone for a clip of Pancetta's sending off.

A look of disbelief, then horror came over Pancetta's face. 'What is this? Why am I . . . I . . .?' His mouth fell open in shock 'NO! Is horrible!' he wailed.

Harry felt really sorry for him. 'And Mauro, look at this.' He showed Moldi the disastrous game.

'I can't look!' he moaned, pushing Harry's phone away.

The other players passed the phone around and you could almost see a light of realisation come into their eyes.

'I think it's working!' said Jake. 'Look at their faces.'

The players were shaking their heads as though waking from a daydream.

'The last thing I remember,' said Slouch 'was being collected by a chauffeur for an interview somewhere.'

'Hey! Zat is exactly what happened to me,' Pancetta agreed.

'You see,' said Harry, 'Antovich kidnapped you and is keeping you here while the robots play instead!'

'We *have* to get out of here,' said Bobbolin. '*Now!*'

'Follow me,' said Harry.

He and Jake raced up the basement stairs followed by twelve international football players. At the top of the stairs, he punched in the code.

Nothing happened.

'Try again!' said Jake, trying not to panic.

'It doesn't work,' Harry said. 'It must have been disabled.'

Just then, the huge screen came back on and it was filled with Anton Antovich's face.

The players turned as one, and walked trance-like back down the stairs.

'So,' said Antovich, 'Super Soccer Boy, I see. What a pleasure to meet you.'

'Antovich! Let them go!' said Harry.

'Now why would I want to do that? And you have interrupted their conditioning, so I will have to keep their robot doubles in circulation a little longer. As for you and your friend, well I think the time has come to try out my junior version. MWAAAHAHAHAHA!'

Jake looked really scared.

'But for now, I have to leave you locked up here. I'm off to see my team win their semi-final. Ah, sweet victory! I can almost smell you.'

The screen switched back to the swirl. There was silence as the players were transfixed once more.

Jake's stomach rumbled really loudly. So loudly that Pancetta turned around, and awoke from his trance-like state before it had time to get a proper hold.

'It must be nearly dinnertime,' Jake said vaguely.

'That's a point,' said Harry. 'How do you get your food?'

'It comes down that chute and through a serving hatch. It's a sort of conveyor belt,' said Slouch.

Harry looked at Jake and smiled slyly. Jake smiled back. They both looked at Ron.

* * *

'Tell me again why we are a-sending da rodent up da chute,' said Pancetta.

'Ron is going to see if there's a way out,' explained Harry for the third time. Not all of the players were that bright. 'If he comes back with something, there might be a way out.'

'A bit like Noah's Ark and the dove,' said Jake, helpfully.

'Eh? You have a bird also? I do not see a bird,' said another player.

Harry sighed. 'Never mind. Up you go, Ron.'

They waited in silence for what seemed like ages, but was in fact only five minutes, and then out popped Ron with half a loaf of French bread.

'Excellent!' said Harry. 'OK. I'll go first, after Ron.'

Harry climbed into the chute and, one by one, the others followed. It was very dark inside and Harry was a bit worried that some of the bigger players might get stuck.

After only a couple of minutes, Harry called back relieved. 'Look, everyone! I can see daylight!'

Chapter Twelve

The Great Escape

When they reached the top of the chute, Harry poked his phone out and took a picture to see what was outside. The kitchen was filled with the silver-coloured robots that he and Jake had seen earlier. They were preparing the evening meal.

'Well, it's a kitchen, not surprisingly,' Harry said. Then he looked serious. 'But it's manned by robots.'

'That explains the awful food,' sneered Slouch.

'OK, now very, very quietly, climb out of the chute and line up against the wall. The door's on the far side of the room.'

Getting twelve burly football players to be quiet is a bit of an ask, thought Jake.

Surprisingly, though, they all managed to climb out without alerting the robots.

It turned out that was the easy part. Harry beckoned for them to follow and then the trouble began. They all tried to follow in a rush and in the confusion, Tortellini managed to knock over a whole trolley full of cutlery.

'Oh no!' he said. To be honest he couldn't have created much more noise if he'd tried.

Every robot in the entire room turned and looked straight at them. Then their eyes began to flash red.

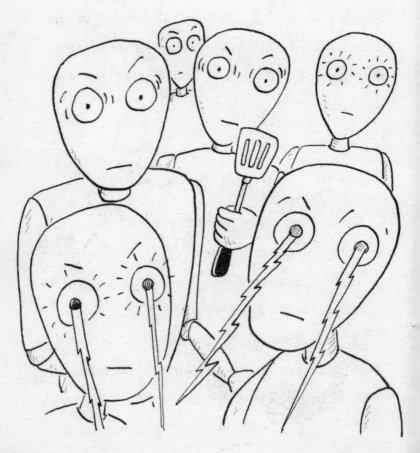

'That can't be good,' whispered Harry.

It wasn't. The robots advanced towards the escapees as a wall, and sparks of electricity shot from their eyes.

'Tasers!' shouted Harry. He grabbed the football out of his backpack and launched an almighty kick at the head of the robot in the centre of the advancing wall. Its head spun around, wobbled slightly and one of the eyes went out.

'Again! Again!' yelled Jake.

'No more footballs!' said Harry.

'Here!' said Pancetta, and threw him a big green cabbage.

BOOOOF! Bits of cabbage leaf flew through the air and the robot's head went with them.

'Everyone! Go for their heads!' yelled Harry. 'Kick anything you can find.'

For five minutes, the kitchen was filled with flying food, bowls, bottles of oil, tins – and robots' heads. When they were down to the last two robots, Harry picked up one of the heads and kicked it through the window, smashing the glass into a million pieces.

'Let's go!' he said.

There was a huge cheer from the players and they all leapt out of the window and onto the grass outside.

'OK,' said Jake. 'What now?!'

'We have to get to the game and expose Antovich's plan,' said Harry. 'But how we get there is a whole different problem.'

'Er, Harry,' said Bobbolin. 'There's a helicopter over there.'

'Yes, we know. It belongs to Antovich.'

'Why don't we use that?' he asked.

'I may be Super Soccer Boy, but I'm afraid I

don't know how to fly just yet,' said Harry.

'But I do, my friend,' said Bobbolin. 'I got my licence last year. I have my own helicopter, you know,' he boasted.

'FANTASTIC!' said Harry. 'Come on, then, Captain Bobbolin, get that baby in the air!'

Everybody piled into the helicopter. It was rather a tight squeeze, but no one wanted to be left behind. In minutes they were airborne and on their way to Wembley.

'Mind the arch!' yelled Harry.

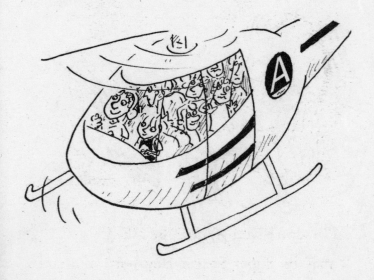

'Is fine, don't worry,' said Bobbolin as he headed for the pitch, scattering players, officials and photographers, and astonishing the crowd.

The helicopter landed gently, right on the centre circle and Harry, Jake and the players poured out.

RUN FOR YOUR LIVES!

If the crowd had been astonished before, they were flabbergasted when they saw who was emerging from the helicopter.

The television commentator was lost for words. 'I ... don't know ... er ... a ... helicopter has landed in the middle of the pitch. And who is that? Pancetta, Moldi and Slouch are all getting out. What is going on?'

There was even more amazement when Tortellini got out of the helicopter – the crowd thought that Tortellini was already on the pitch!

Harry looked up at the royal box. There was Antovich. He'd realised what was happening and was trying to escape from the ground. Harry grabbed the match ball and with a tremendous kick, he aimed it straight at Antovich. 'You're not leaving!' Harry shouted.

Antovich went flying. *'Urrgggh!'* *Crunch!*

'Let's get him, boys,' said Pancetta.

The twelve former soccer prisoners ran to the stand, picked Antovich up and carried him back down to the pitch.

Pancetta grabbed a microphone. 'Ladies and gentlemen,' he began, 'this is the man responsible for everything that has gone wrong in zis tournament. He is a disgrace to football.'

Antovich hid his head in shame.

The police arrived and led him away. He was booed off the pitch by the entire Wembley crowd. Harry *almost* felt sorry for him.

Extra Time

After the revelations, FC Skronto were disqualified, and the tournament was officially abandoned. As the final hadn't taken place, the kidnapped players played a friendly match against the winners of the other semi. Harry and Jake were guests of honour. They were both in the official photographs with the teams and Harry even got to play the last five minutes on

the pitch. Not only that, but he scored a brilliant
goal.

At the end of the match, Pancetta came up to
Harry. 'This is for you!' he said.

Harry looked at the match ball. It had been signed by all the players on the pitch.

'Thanks, Emilio,' said Harry, thrilled to bits.

HARRY'S F⚽⚽TBALL FACTS!

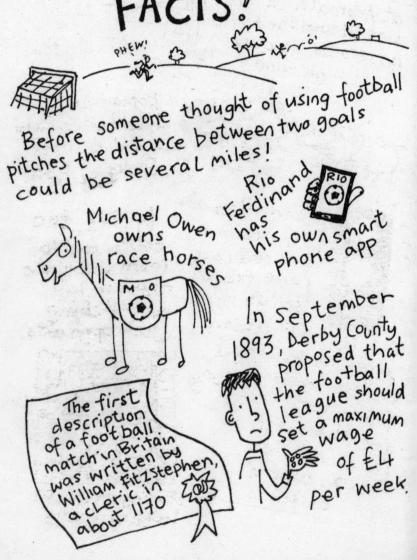

PHEW!

Before someone thought of using football pitches the distance between two goals could be several miles!

Michael Owen owns race horses

M O

Rio Ferdinand has his own smart phone app

RIO

In September 1893, Derby County proposed that the football league should set a maximum wage of £4 per week.

The first description of a football match in Britain was written by William Fitzstephen, a cleric in about 1170

Dundee Utd's Premier Reserve League game v Dunfermline at Arbroath in 1998 was abandoned after 90 seconds because of high winds

Romanian midfielder Ion Radu was sold in 1998 for 500kg of Pork!

The idea of yellow and red cards came from British ref Ken Aston when he watched traffic lights changing. They were used for the first time in the 1970 world cup.

In 1973, the entire Galilee team spent the night in jail for kicking their opponents

during an Israeli league game

Join
Super Soccer Boy
online:

www.supersoccerboy.com

⚽ Fun activities
⚽ Football facts and quiz
⚽ All the latest
on the books
⚽ And much more!